Mattland

Mattland

story by
Hazel Hutchins
and Gail Herbert
art by **Dušan Petričić**

annick press
toronto + new york + vancouver

Matt had moved three times with his family and this was the worst place of all.

There were no climbing trees, just scraggly pines.
There was no one he knew, just houses with closed doors.
There was barely any grass. Everywhere was mud and water.
Across the wetness lay only scattered building scraps, a few
rocks, and a stick.

Matt picked up the stick. He felt like breaking it. He felt like throwing it. He felt like hitting something with it. But the stick felt comfortable in his hand and, instead, Matt drew a line in the mud.

Rain had fallen that morning. The earth was full to overflowing and the line filled with water. It was squiggly, like lines on the map his parents showed him each time they moved. He gave the line a squiggly name.

"Snake River," he said.

He connected the line to a puddle. The puddle was rounded in the middle and bumpy at the ends. "Turtle Lake," said Matt.

He moved some rocks into a jagged row. He could
have named them the Rockies, like the real mountains,
but he didn't. These peaks needed a name of their own.
"Dog Tooth Mountains," he said.

A huge puddle became the Far Off Ocean. A great flat area, where tufts of grass were trying to push upwards, became the Buffalo Grasslands. In between was a clump of earth that Matt smoothed into a round hill. He stood on Old Baldy and looked down.

"Mattland," he said.

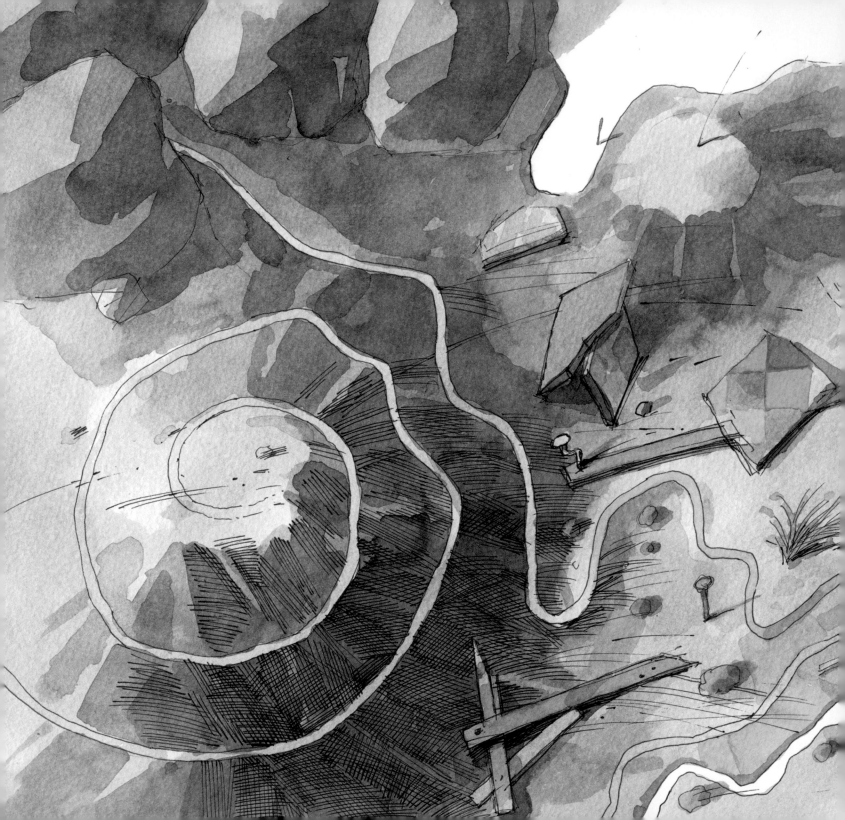

The scraps in the mud looked different now. Matt gathered them into a pile. He used a block of wood to smooth a winding ribbon down from the mountains.

"Far-From-Home Road," said Matt.

Sticks became a farmhouse, a piece of tin a barn. Fuzzy seeds became sheep in the pasture. He was just plucking a seventh sheep from his sock when he noticed something that had not been there before.

An outsider had arrived in Mattland.

She had not been invited. She had
not asked if she could enter. For a long
time Matt stood looking at her.

Finally, she reached out a hand.
Resting in her open palm was a single
Popsicle stick. She handed it to Matt
and walked away.

The stick became fence posts for Burr-Berry farm.
The road began to wind along the water. Animal tracks
appeared where deer came to drink. Here and there a hill
was born. Culverts were needed to cross small streams.
At Snake River something larger was needed.

Split-shingle Bridge was even better than he'd planned. Soon tiny houses, stores, and a factory appeared along the shore.

And the outsider was back with four pine cones and an empty berry container.

Matt had been hoping the Turtle Lakers would have a baseball diamond on which to play. Behind the park he planted prickly trees. The leftover bits made an interesting pattern on the earth, and soon the Pine Needle Railway Line raced across the flats.

This time when the outsider returned, she needed both hands to hold all she had found.

The bones, weathered clean and white as wood, were buried for future explorers in the Dinosaur Badlands. The broken key became the Mount Fang Weather Station. The flattened penny became a landing pad for UFOs ... just in case. Colored pebbles, bits of tile, and ends of string each found a place, just as the rain began to fall once more.

Almost instantly, Snake River filled to overflowing.
Culverts clogged with mud. A surge of water threatened
the bridge. Matt and the outsider rushed to save things,
but all was about to be lost, when suddenly …

… help arrived from unexpected places. Steadily they worked. Soon dams, dikes, and deep canals were guiding the water safely away.

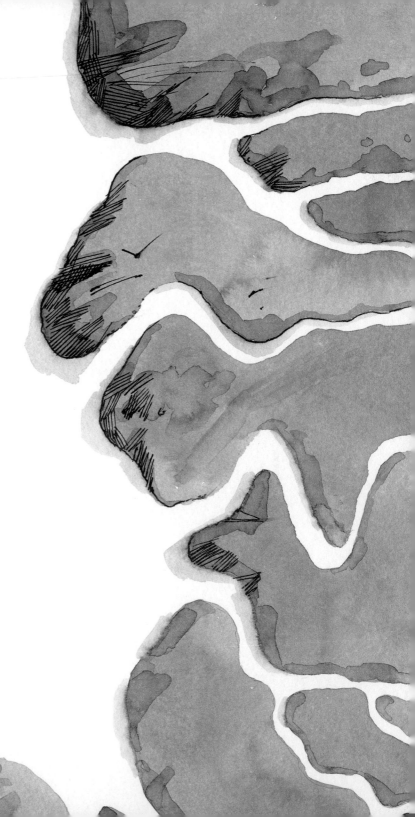

The rain stopped. The water calmed. The sky cleared.

And shining boats appeared on Turtle Lake.

We acknowledge the support of the Canada Council for the Arts, the Ontario Arts Council, and the Government
of Canada through the Book Publishing Industry Development Program (BPIDP) for our publishing activities.

ONTARIO ARTS COUNCIL
CONSEIL DES ARTS DE L'ONTARIC

Cataloging in Publication

Hutchins, H. J. (Hazel J.)
    Mattland / story by Hazel Hutchins and Gail Herbert ; art by Dušan Petričić.

ISBN 978-1-55451-121-1 (bound).—ISBN 978-1-55451-120-4 (pbk.)

    I. Herbert, Gail II. Petričić, Dušan III. Title.

PS8565.U826M38 2008   jC813'.54   C2007-906533-3

Distributed in Canada by:
Firefly Books Ltd.
66 Leek Crescent
Richmond Hill, ON
L4B 1H1

Published in the U.S.A. by:
Annick Press (U.S.) Ltd.
Distributed in the U.S.A. by:
Firefly Books (U.S.) Inc.
P.O. Box 1338
Ellicott Station
Buffalo, NY 14205

Printed in China.

Visit Annick at: www.annickpress.com
Visit Hazel at: www.telusplanet.net/public/hjhutch

For Jessica, Arden and Chris.
—G.H. and H.H.

For all displaced children.
—D.P.